Notes to Parents and Teachers:

As a child becomes more familiar reading books, it is important for them to rely on and use reading strategies more independently to help figure out words they do not know.

REMEMBER: PRAISE IS A GREAT MOTIVATOR!

Here are some praise points for beginning readers:

- I saw you get your mouth ready to say the first letter of that word.
- I like the way you used the picture to help you figure out that word.
- I noticed that you saw some sight words you knew how to read!

Book Ends for the Reader!

Here are some reminders before reading the text:

- Point to each word you read to make it match what you say.

- Use the picture for help.

- Look at and say the first letter sound of the word.

- Look for sight words that you know how to read in the story.

- Think about the story to see what word might make sense.

Words to Know Before You Read

bad

cake

hot

mad

out

pot

runs

song

Kate is so, so Mad!

A Story About Angry Feelings

BY
R. E. ROBERTSON

ILLUSTRATED BY
DANIELA DOGLIANI

Educational Media

A Division of
Carson
Dellosa
Education

The cake is ruined.

This is bad!

Kate is

so

Her face is red. Her words are hot.

Kate feels like

A

BOILING

POT!

She hops. She kicks. She wants to SCREAM!

She feels full of swirling steam.

Kate runs outside. She hits the ground.

She yanks a weed, twists it round and round.

"Relax," Gramps says.
"Breathe in, breathe out."

14

Kate's eyes water. Tears come out.

Gramps hugs Kate. He hums a song.

Kate hugs Gramps. She hums along.

Kate cools down. She knows what to do.

"Can we bake cupcakes, me and you?"

They clean the mess.
They go to the store.

Kate is not angry anymore.

Book Ends for the Reader

I know...

1. What made Kate mad?
2. Who did Kate see outside?
3. What did Gramps tell Kate to do?

I think...

1. Why did Kate feel like a boiling pot?
2. Did Kate's brother mean to make Kate mad?
3. What are some things you do to cool down when you are mad?

Book Ends for the Reader

What happened in this book?

Look at each picture and talk about what happened in the story.

About the Author

R. E. Robertson is an author and nature lover. His favorite pastimes include reading, cooking, camping, and spending time with his wife, children, and grandchildren.

About the Illustrator

Daniela Dogliani is a children's book illustrator based in Turin, Italy. Since childhood, she's been a passionate doodler and bookworm. She studied at the Academy of Fine Arts of Turin and graduated with an MSc in Visual Arts and Communication.

Library of Congress PCN Data

Kate is so, SO Mad! (A Story About Angry Feelings) /
R.E. Robertson
(Playing and Learning Together)
ISBN 978-1-73160-591-7 (hard cover)(alk. paper)
ISBN 978-1-73160-427-9 (soft cover)
ISBN 978-1-73160-644-0 (e-Book)
ISBN 978-1-73160-664-8 (ePub)
Library of Congress Control Number: 2018967563

Rourke Educational Media
Printed in the United States of America
04-2272211937

© 2020 Rourke Educational Media

www.rourkeeducationalmedia.com

Edited by: Kim Thompson
Layout by: Kathy Walsh
Cover and interior illustrations by: Daniela Dogliani